ALL BY MYSELF
BY
MERCER MAYER

♘ **A GOLDEN BOOK • NEW YORK**

Golden Books Publishing Company, Inc., New York, New York 10106

I can get out of bed
all by myself.

I can button
my overalls.

I can brush my fur.

I can put on my socks…

and tie my shoes.

I can pour some juice
for my little sister…

and help her eat breakfast.

I can pull a duck for her.

I can drive my truck.

I can kick my ball...

and roll on the ground.

I can pound with my hammer.

I can sail my boat.

I can look after
my little sister.

I can help Dad
trim a bush…

or ice a cake for Mom.

I can look at a
book and find
a mouse.

I can color a picture.

I can put my toys away…

and get into my pajamas.

I can brush my teeth.

I can put myself to bed...

but I can't go to sleep
without a story.

Good night.

10.95
8/01